Window

Jeannie Baker

Greenwillow Books, New York

I am grateful to Haydn Washington, biologist and
environmental writer and consultant, for his help.

The artwork was prepared as collage
constructions, which were reproduced
in full color from photographs by
David Cummings. The cover art was
photographed by Murray Van Der Veer.
The text type is Simoncini Garamond.

Manufactured in China by
South China Printing Company Ltd.
First Edition   12

Library of Congress
Cataloging-in-Publication Data
Baker, Jeannie.
Window / by Jeannie Baker.   p.   cm.
Summary: Chronicles the events and changes
in a young boy's life and in his environment,
from babyhood to grownup, through wordless
scenes observed from the window of his room.
ISBN 0-688-08917-8 (trade).
ISBN 0-688-08918-6 (lib.)
[1. Stories without words.   2. Ecology—
Australia—Fiction.   3. Australia—Fiction.]
I. Title.   PZ7.B1742Wi   1991
[E]—dc 20   90-3922   CIP   AC

To Rodney, Haydn, and David

We are changing the face of our world at an
alarming and an increasing pace.

From the present rates of destruction, we
can estimate that by the year 2020 no wilderness
will remain on our planet, outside that protected
in national parks and reserves.

By the same year 2020, a quarter of our present
plant and animal species will be extinct if we continue
at the current growing pace of change.

Already, at least two species become extinct each hour.

Our planet is changing before our eyes. However,
by understanding and changing the way we personally
affect the environment, we can make a difference.

JEANNIE BAKER was born in England and now lives in Australia. Since 1972 she has worked on her collage constructions, many of which are designed to illustrate picture books but stand individually as works of art. They are part of many public art collections and have been exhibited in galleries in London, New York, and throughout Australia.

Jeannie Baker is the author-artist of a number of distinguished picture books. Among them are *Home in the Sky*, an ALA Notable Book, and *Where the Forest Meets the Sea,* a *Boston Globe-Horn Book* Honor Book and the recipient of an IBBY Honor Award and a Friends of the Earth Award in Great Britain. *Where the Forest Meets the Sea* has also been made into an animated film directed by Ms. Baker.

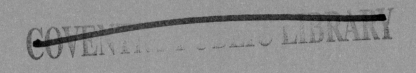